This book
belongs to:

_____

_____

This edition first published in Great Britain by HarperCollins Publishers Ltd in 2000

1 3 5 7 9 10 8 6 4 2

Copyright © 2000 Enid Blyton Ltd. Enid Blyton's signature mark and the words
"NODDY" and "TOYLAND" are Registered Trade Marks of Enid Blyton Ltd.
For further information on Enid Blyton please contact www.blyton.com

ISBN: 0 00 710788 9

Reproduction by Graphic Studio S.r.l. Verona
Printed in Italy by Garzanti Verga S.r.l.

Bumpy Dog Helps Out

Collins

An imprint of HarperCollinsPublishers

It was a
bright, sunny
morning in Toyland.
Bumpy Dog was playing with a stick in the garden.
He tossed it into the air. Then he kicked it across the
lawn. He even tried to balance it on his nose. But he
decided that it really
wasn't much
fun playing
by himself.

He ran into the house to find Tessie Bear. Perhaps she would play with him!

"Oh, Bumpy Dog," said Tessie Bear when she saw him.

"I have to finish knitting a jumper for Noddy, but I've lost one of my knitting needles. Have you been playing with it?" Bumpy Dog shook his head.

Then he remembered the stick he had in his mouth. That was long and pointed, and looked very much like a knitting needle. Perhaps Tessie Bear could use that. He dropped the stick at her feet.

"Bumpy Dog!" shouted Tessie crossly. "I am far too busy to play. Go out into the garden and take your dirty stick with you."

Bumpy Dog didn't like Tessie Bear getting cross with him. Especially when he had only been trying to help.

The sound of Noddy's car cheered Bumpy up.
Perhaps Noddy would play with him. Bumpy
jumped up and barked at Noddy over the
garden gate.

Instead of being pleased to see him, Noddy looked very cross.

"I am in a hurry, Bumpy Dog," he grumbled. "I promised to help Mr Tubby Bear in his garden."

Noddy's car was filled with plants and soil and garden tools.

"Mr Tubby will wonder where I have got to," said Noddy. "Do try to stay out of mischief, Bumpy Dog."

As he drove away, some long runner-bean canes fell from the back of his car.

CLATTER!

Bumpy Dog leapt over
the gate and picked up the
canes in his mouth. He would
help Noddy by taking them to
Mr Tubby Bear's house. Bumpy Dog
ran as fast as he could after Noddy's car.

Suddenly, Mr Plod appeared. Bumpy Dog tried to run past the policeman. But the canes he was carrying were so long that they banged into him and knocked Mr Plod to the ground.

OUCH!

"Right, Bumpy Dog," said the policeman angrily.
"I will have to arrest you for assaulting me."
    He felt in his pocket.

"Where's my special police pencil?" he asked.
"I need it to write down the details in my special
police notebook."

Bumpy Dog thought he should help Mr Plod find his pencil. He dropped the canes on the ground and began to sniff around. He sniffed Mr Plod's pockets. He sniffed around Mr Plod's feet.

He sniffed until he found
Mr Plod's pencil which had
fallen on the pavement!
He picked it up in his
mouth and gave it
to the policeman.

"Now I can arrest you, Bumpy Dog!" said Mr Plod.
But Bumpy had already run off with the canes
towards Mr Tubby Bear's house.

As Bumpy got nearer to the house, he saw Noddy and Mr Tubby Bear standing by Noddy's car. They were both scratching their heads.

"Where can those canes have got to?" wondered Mr Tubby Bear. "I need them to make my runner-beans grow up tall and strong."

"Ah! Here they are," he laughed when he saw Bumpy Dog running towards them. At least Mr Tubby Bear seemed happy to see Bumpy. But Noddy was not very happy at all.

"You bad dog," he shouted. "You stole those canes on purpose didn't you?"

Bumpy Dog dropped the canes on the ground and began to cry. He had only been trying to help and now Noddy was cross with him too.

Bumpy Dog walked home sadly. Everybody seemed to be getting cross with him.

When he arrived back at Tessie Bear's house, he quietly crept inside.

"Bumpy Dog! Where have you been?" cried Tessie Bear when she saw him. "I've been so worried about you!"

Bumpy was so glad that Tessie was no longer cross with him that he leapt up to lick her face and accidentally pushed her over.

She fell back into the armchair, and CLINK!
Something fell out underneath. It was Tessie's lost
knitting needle!

"You clever dog!" Tessie laughed, hugging
her pet. "I am going to buy you a nice juicy bone to
say thank you!"

Tessie and Bumpy Dog
went into Toy Town to buy
the bone. Who should they
meet there but Noddy! He had
bought a bone too.

"I didn't know you had a dog,
Noddy," said Tessie Bear.

Before he could reply, Mr Plod
appeared. He was also
carrying a bone.
Bumpy Dog sniffed
all the bones.

"Don't do that,
Bumpy, they're not
all for you!" laughed
Tessie Bear.

"Oh, but they are," said Noddy and Mr Plod together.

"You carried the canes that I had dropped, didn't you, Bumpy?" said Noddy. "I'm sorry I got cross with you."

"And you helped me find my special police pencil too," said Mr Plod.

Bumpy Dog now had *three* bones.
He happily began to gobble
them up. If he always got
rewards like this, he
would try to help
out more often!

THE END

Here are some more books for you to enjoy:

Noddy's Bumper Activity Book
ISBN: 0-00-710640-8

Noddy's Bumper Colouring Book
ISBN: 0-00-710639-4

The Goblins and the Ice Cream
ISBN: 0-00-710786-2

Mr Plod's Bossy Day
ISBN: 0-00-710789-7

Mr Straw's New Cow
ISBN: 0-00-710787-0

Noddy's and the Runaway Cakes
ISBN: 0-00-710637-8

Noddy's Special Whistle
ISBN: 0-00-710638-6